The JOURNAL of ETIENNE MERCIER

Queen Charlotte Islands

1853

Text by DAVID BOUCHARD
Paintings by GORDON MILLER

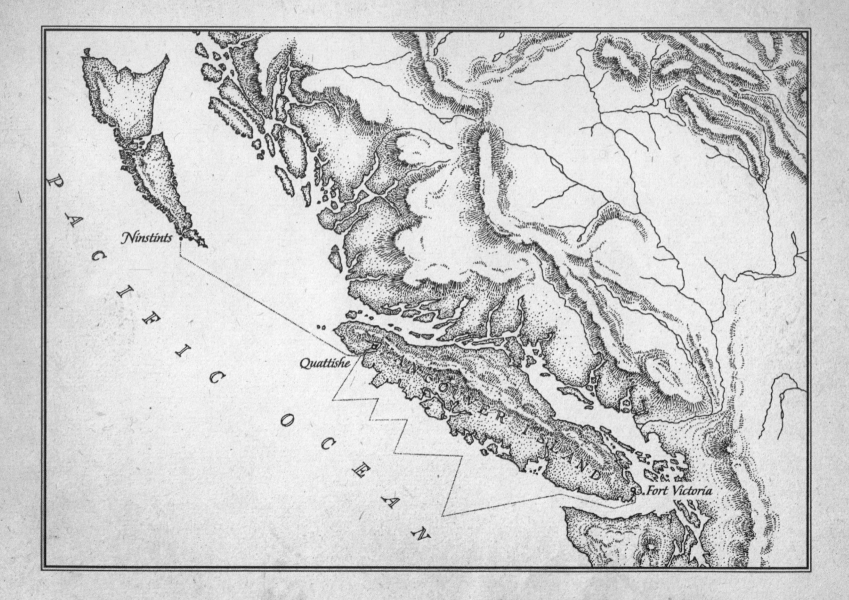

Ninstints

Quattishe

PACIFIC OCEAN

VANCOUVER ISLAND

Fort Victoria

Mon Journal

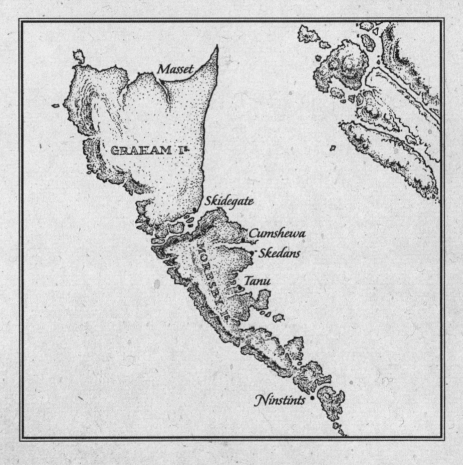

Queen Charlotte Islands

1853

Cher Journal,

You know me, but in case of the event that something happen to me, my name is Etienne Mercier.

I am from Robertval, dans les banlieux de Chicoutimi, and I have work for la Compagnie de la Baie d'Hudson for six year now.

I am 28 year old. I am almos six foot and I weigh 18 stone. My hair is brown. My eyes is brown. I have 15 brother and sister. I am Catholique and I love the animal.

I have been a voyageur, a trappeur, a coureur de bois and other thing. Today, I don't know what I am, only that the Compagnie is pay me to travel up the Queen Charlotte to write what I see. He want to see how different the Indian here is to the Indian back home. This will not be difficult because he is different in the way he talk, he sing, he dance, in the way he make the lodge, the totem, the canoe, everything. Just wait Journal! You will hear about it and you will see it in the picture.

I am lucky that I can write and I am lucky too that I can make the picture. For mos my life, I make the picture for no one to see. One day my frien, petit Jean Latour, he's fine one of my picture and show it to my patron, Monsieur James Douglas. Eh bien, Monsieur Douglas like the picture and me, I am get this great job. Who would have believe?

I have wait here in Fort Victoria for the schooner to take me north. I can visit my frien on the Queen Charlotte. Do you know, Journal, where the name Charlotte come from? It sound French, I know, but it is English. It is the name of the ship of Capitain Dixon who is one of the firs white to see those Island, maybe one hundred year ago.

I was up there las year when la Compagnie was worry that the problem will come if the American hear about gold on those Island. Gold!?! It should not take gold to get people up there. It is the mos beautiful land in the world. The animal, the fish and the tree is bigger, stronger and more beautiful than anywhere I have seen. Wait until you see!

I have travel many mile in my canoe. I should have no trouble with it. The Indian know me. He is my frien. I should have no trouble with him. I have food and drink. I am not expect to have any trouble unless the weather is like it was las year, when I lose my frien Clément.

I am very happy to accept this job for all the reason and for the chance to fine Clément. I miss him very much.

Etienne Mercier

March 21, 1853

Ah! Journal! Quelle chance!!!

Our firs day and guess what I fine last night in Quattishe?
The Winter Dance!

In Québec, we celebrate le Carnaval. Here, to get through the long, rainy winter, the Indian have the Winter Dance. I have never seen it until las night. I can believe my good luck.

I had been on the schooner many day. I was very tired so when I was invite to that dance, I almos refuse. Thank God I didn't.

I walk into a long house that is fill with all the village people and a few invite gues like me. I have walk into another world. Somewhere, mix in with the sound of moaning, crying and chanting, I hear the drum. No one seem to notice me and yet I am stand there, in the glow of the fire. I smell the meat and the fish and the burning cedar. For the nex six hour, I am entertain by the Kwakiutl. We eat. He tell story. He dance. That long house is fill with history, spirit and magique. In fac, those Indian call winter Tseska. That mean supernatural.

I watch the Hamatsa, the bird monster. Those Raven, Huxwhukw and Galukwani (crooked beak) live in the sky and feed on people. That dance is frighten and yet spectaculaire! I can hardly believe he is not real! Jus look at the picture Journal!

Père Lacombe, he is a good man but he is not excite like those Hamatsa. I am anxious to tell him about that ceremony an show him the picture.

I like to sing as I paddle my canoe and today I sing one of my favorite song, Les Raftsmen. No sign of Clément yet, but I think of him often las night during that dance.

> Là où ce qu'ils sont our frien out here
> Là où ce qu'ils sont our frien out here
> That we might be de bons amis
> Bing sur la ring, bang sur la rang
> Sur la terre and on the sea
> Bing sur la ring bing bang —

I am singing in Franglais since three year now when the wife of my patron travel with us and ask to learn the song. At firs, I did it for her. Now, I do it for me. I like it.

Etienne Mercier
March 30, 1853

Cher Journal,

We have reach Ninstints, the firs village at the bottom of those Island.

Ninstints is the main village of the Kunghit Haida. I love all the totem
in front of the seventeen long house I have count. Mon Journal,
what do you think will happen to those totem in year to come?

Ninstints is open to the sea, so mos ship from Europe stop
here. I don't know why, but today there is none.
Only our schooner.

The English is careful about the way he
trade with the Indian, but the American is
frien with him and with us Canadien too.
In fac, it was because one of those
American ship offer me a sail to Fort
Victoria las year when the weather was bad,
that I loose Clément.

I was thinking that he would leave anyway to start a family or maybe just to go back
to his own. I wonder if he will remember me if I fine him? Jus in case, I have pack
some extra bannock. That is his favorite food. I learn how to make it from the Cree.

Today, I am singing C'est l'Aviron.

M'en revenant de north of Fort Victoria
M'en revenant de north of Fort Victoria
I was alone, Je ne sais où était Clément
C'est l'aviron that can take me back to fine him
Stroke after stroke, il me mène en haut.

Etienne Mercier
April 3, 1853

Cher Journal,

We have make good time, you and me. We are already at Tanu.

I have spend some time with that young carver who prepare a pole for the chief.

Today I will make the picture of Tanu, then I will finish the picture I start
las year when I was up north in Klukwan. I have been think about it since
that dance in Quattishe.

Las winter when we were in Klukwan, me and Clément, I was invite
to a celebration of the Tlingit. By luck, we got there during a potlatch
(an by good luck too, I got a new knife).

White people can learn from the Indian, Journal. Can you imagine that
to impress your frien and your enemy too, you invite him to a party and give
him gift? The Indian have such a party. He call it potlatch. In la Compagnie, potlatch
mean trade, but the Indian have use that Chinook word since the firs flood.
It mean present.

To be an artist is a honorable thing for the Indian (maybe that is why he like me, because I make the picture). The more north I have travel, the more beautiful the art I have seen. In that long house at Klukwan, I saw a wonderful picture "Rain Screen". It show how this proud people defend that village for year agains the Russian.

That potlatch was to celebrate the marriage of the chief daughter. It was going on for three week already. I am not sure who she was marry but he mus be important because it was a big one.

The potlatch happen at the most interesting time too, Journal. I have heard about a war between two tribe that had to be stop for a potlatch. The canoe that was fill with weapon had to be empty and fill with gift, because one of the chief was invite his enemy to his potlatch. Nobody can refuse such an invitation because he is very proud. Not only will he go, but he will remember everything that is done for him and everything that is give to him, so that he can outdo his enemy when it is his turn for the potlatch.

This is a good way for the rich to share. At home, the rich give to the church and the church help the one that does not have. Me, I like the potlatch, Journal. When I go home to Québec, I will do it.

My father has taught me Sur le Pont d'Avignon. Do you know it, Journal? It is an old song from before la Révolution Française. People were hang from that pont in Avignon?

Sur le pont d'Avignon
I got a knife as a present
Un couteau, très nouveau
From that potlatch I did go?

Etienne Mercier
April 6, 1853

Cher Journal,

What a merveilleux way to begin the day.

It is not everyday that a man is lucky enough to paddle nex to the giant fish, but this morning coming into Skedans, I was. I lay my paddle down, and for a long time, I jus sit and watch.

A family of eight or more of the big one appear out of the mis traveling south, while me, I am going north. They are quiet like the Haida war party and if they seem gentle, they are not. I have seen them hunt!

I have seen two, probably a mother and father, throw a lion de mer of maybe 50 stone, high in the air like the small child who play with his food. They did this again and again so that the baby will learn how to hunt and kill.

I have seen one of the giant fish fly through the air and land on the shore behind a hundred seal. I have watch him roll back toward the sea, knocking many seal into the water where the other big fish wait.

I have often said that everything here in the ouest is big — the mountain, the tree and the bear and nothing is bigger than this fish, this killing fish. Of all the beauty here, there is little I will miss more than the excitement of sharing water with him.

I sing extra loud so Clément can hear me if he is near. He is not a good singer that Clément, but he love the musique and En Roulant ma Boule En Roulant is his favourite song.

En roulant ma boule en roulant
Where he is, I do not know?

I spend two week looking for him.
En roulant ma boule!
The sea, the coast an inland too,
Roulie, roulant, ma boule en roulant

En roulant ma boule en roulant
Where he is, I do not know???

Etienne Mercier
April 8, 1853

Cher Journal,

From Lac St. Jean, through the prairie and then the mountain, I have seen many Indian village.

The prairie Indian move often. He is fas to pack his house and all his thing. For some Indian, having thing is not important. But for the Haida, it is. His fur, blanket, canoe, mask, and his house is all important to him. The Haida might be happy in Victoria because so many there are like that. They like having nice thing.

The Haida live in long house, up to fifty in one house. He decorate his house with picture and with totem pole. He paint his house and the pole to show how rich he is and to bring honour to his family.

You know too how rich is a village by counting the number of totem and by looking at the picture on the house.

I spend las night is Cumshewa (the name come from the chief Gomshewa). That village is much like other village with those long house line up on the beach. This morning at low tide, I went for a walk to look for Clément. I have heard that an islet separate that village from the burial ground and an old fort. Clément would like that. He might go there.

These people are happy to see me. They like it when I make the picture of their village. They ask me to stay longer. I have too much to do. I said non.

I only stay las night and this morning I leave to Vive la Canadienne!

> Vive la Canadienne
> Paddle, paddle, paddle round the land
> Looking for my frien Clément
> Hoping he's look for me too.

Etienne Mercier
April 10, 1853

Wake up Journal! Hurry, Réveille!!!

Quiet! Quiet! I have been hide here for one hour. It is jus after sunrise. Like other morning, I am on the water early when, from I don't know where, I hear the war chant. I immediately get very quiet and paddle hard toward those bush. The war canoe with maybe 25 brave pass right by me, no more than 100 feet. I am so scare! I have not move for one hour.

You should have seen it, Journal. The brave is all paint for battle. I saw no head, no blood and no capture slave, so I know that he is still look for trouble. The prairie Indian take the scalp (the head is too big to carry). The Haida take the whole head. He tie it to the side of his canoe and take it home to put on the pole for all to see.

That Haida spend much of his time making war. Sometime he fight for revenge, sometime for anger and sometime to keep his neighbor from making war on him. He might attack that neighbour, kill all the people and take several head back to his village to put on the pole. The message say, "Do not come near me because I am dangerous!" One day I saw, on a pole, a head that look like my frien Adrien Bouchard. I did not look very long? It was probably jus somebody who look like him (but I have not seen Adrien for a long time now!).

Me, I know not to make the Indian mad. I know too that jus because I have not
made him mad does not mean he will not be mad. He has a long memory. He will
take revenge on one white for what another did. This happen at Nootka when
Chief Maquinna was killing the crew of the ship Boston. Even if he can be kind
and fair, you mus always be careful of him.

After this morning, I thank God that I am Catholique and that Clément is not here.
My frien does not know when to be quiet.

Et Journal, how about A la Claire Fontaine? Do you know it? I like those word?

> A la Claire Fontaine
> Not out here on the sea
> Je trouve l'eau si belle
> Clément my frien and me.
>
> Il y a longtemps que je t'aime
> Clément! Where can my frien be?

April 14, 1853

Etienne Mercier

Cher Journal,

Everybody love the eagle. Everybody except Clément.

I see the eagle everywhere on the Queen Charlotte. There is no bird like him and to see him, you will think he is fierce. But he is not, not like the big fish. He feed mos on dead fish, shell fish and dead animal and the Indian love this bird.

The Haida is divide into two clan: the eagle and the raven. The village chief is from the bigger clan, eagle or raven. The politique of those clan is difficult and interest. An eagle mus marry an eagle and a raven, a raven. Like us Canadien! I can imagine the face of Père Lacombe if I tell him I am marry a protestant! Seigneur, prends pitié!!!

There is many eagle here in Skidegate.

I am walking on the sand and this big one is flying around me. Maybe he is thinking I am out to hunt or fish and he will get lucky. After some time, he land. Slowly, I move close to him to make the picture. He is watching me but he is not moving. He is staying right there for a long time. I make the picture and while I am make it, I sing "Au Claire de la Lune". He seem to like that!

Au claire de la lune

Une chanson you know

I have no fortune

Mais j'ai mes beaux mots —

Ma chandelle est morte

Now . . . I paint . . . your . . . queue!

This should do jus fine now?

Pour l'amour de Dieu

P.S. I could never make that picture if Clément was here.

Etienne Mercier

April 16, 1853

Journal, you are all wet.

Water is come in the long house las night.

Quelle tempête! What a storm!

I climb on the roof with the other men. We put rock and big branch to hold the roof from blow away. The Indian does not make the long house roof secure because he has to move it for smoke to get out when he make the fire.

I love that storm. It remind me of how strong the sea and sky is.

Journal, did I ever tell you about how genereux the Indian is to stranger? Not jus here in Skidegate, but in all village. When I see smoke come from a house, I open the door and he share whatever he has. That is jus what he does.

Remember when I tell you the Haida might be happy in Victoria? Maybe non! The Haida would be surprise to go to a house in Fort Victoria and ask to share. White people are not so good for share. (Clément him, he is good! Me, I get the food and Clément, he is get a share.)

April 18, 1853
Étienne Mercier

Cher Journal,

A long time ago, man and animal was part of the same family.

This is what the Indian believe. He keep this family alive through the picture, carving and dance. And he keep his heritage through the family emblem. With pride, he show it on his house, his totem, his canoe, everywhere. Jus look at what I saw this morning Journal!

Sometime, the picture is jus too good for word.

> Alouette, gentille Alouette
> Won't you help me
> Fine my frien Clément?
>
> Up where you are, gentille Alouette
> If you see him
> Tell him to come home!

Etienne Mercier
April 30, 1853

Cher Journal,

The sky of Masset is dark and cold.

That village is large and important.

I was lucky to spend las night in "Monster House," the new house of Chief Wiah.
It is the biggest house I have seen on the Queen Charlotte, and the only one I have
seen with full carve corner post. I love that house.

In my picture, it is the one with the two oval door.

I will go to bed early tonight, because tomorrow I start for home, without Clément.
I have give up to fine him.

> Frère Clément, frère Clément
> Where are you? Où es-tu?
> Can you hear me, Clément?
> Can you see me, Clément?
> Ding, dang, dong.
> Ding, dang, dong.

May 10, 1853

Étienne Mercier

Cher Journal,

Sometime, Journal, I wish you could sing with me or better even, paddle with me!
(I'm just joke.)

> Chevalier de la table ronde
> Come an help, paddle my canoe
> We take turn and we work together
> Toi et moi, without dire un mot —
>
> Is your turn? Oui, oui, oui
> Is my turn? Non, non, non
> You can help paddle my canoe
>
> Is your turn? Oui, oui, oui
> Is my turn? Non, non, non
> When we stop, on fera dodo

May 15, 1853

Étienne

Ah Journal,

You will never guess!

Las night, I arrive late back here in Ninstints. I am going home.
I have give up to fine Clément.

I am sleep on the beach under my canoe when I hear that familiar sound.
I throw aside my canoe et voilà! It is him, Clément!

He is sit there in the morning light, every bit as wonderful as I remember him to be.

I immediately realize that I mus study all the sign, because like the Indian, I believe
Clément to be the transformer, the trickster, the magician.

So what is my frien up to?

I see the totem behind him. I examine the long house. Hélas, my eye fall on the canoe he is perch on. Why has Clément choose that one and not another one? Is it because of the picture of the big fish? Those fish live in close family and him and me, we are like a family! We should be together!

What is Clément try to tell me or does he jus want food?

No matter. I will get food then I will come back and do what I should have done two year ago. I will make the picture of my frien Clement.

Etienne Mercier

June 10, 1853

For my son — Etienne Mercier Bouchard — D.B.

I am grateful for this opportunity to acknowledge many years of support from my family.

These paintings exist largely because of the encouragement of Bill McLennan, Dr. George F. MacDonald and Bill Ellis.

Dedicated with love to my mother.

GORDON MILLER

Text copyright © 1998 David Bouchard
Paintings copyright © 1998 Gordon Miller

Orca Book Publishers gratefully acknowledges the support for our publishing programs provided by the following agencies: the Department of Canadian Heritage, the Canada Council for the Arts, and the British Columbia Ministry of Small Business, Tourism and Culture.

Canadian Cataloguing in Publication Data
Bouchard, Dave, 1952-
The journal of Etienne Mercier

ISBN 1-55143-128-9
1. Queen Charlotte Islands (B.C.)—Fiction. 2. Haida Indians—Fiction. 3. Hudson's Bay Company—History—Fiction.
I. Miller, Gordon, 1932- II. Title.
PS8553.O759J68 1998   C813'.54   C97-911107-2
PR9199.3.B617J68 1998

Library of Congress Catalog Card Number: 97-81098

Orca Book Publishers   Orca Book Publishers
PO Box 5626, Station B   PO Box 468
Victoria, BC V8R 6S4   Custer, WA 98240-0468
Canada   USA

Design by Arifin A. Graham, Alaris Design
Historical advice and aged paper by Courtland Benson, Bookbinder
Printed and bound in Canada